A CHRISTMAS STORY

BRIAN WILDSMITH

ALFRED A. KNOPF ❧ NEW YORK

Once, a long time ago in a town called Nazareth,
a little donkey was born.

When the little donkey was almost nine months old, his mother set
out on a long trip with her mistress and master, whose names were

Mary and Joseph. They asked Rebecca, a child who lived nearby, to look after the little donkey while they were gone.

But the little donkey was very sad without his mother and
refused to eat. So Rebecca packed food and water and promised
the little donkey that they would find his mother.

And they set out to follow Mary and Joseph.

The roads were full of people traveling to various towns and cities.
"Have you seen a donkey with a man and a woman?" Rebecca
asked a traveler.
"Yes, they passed me on the road to Jerusalem," the traveler replied.

Rebecca and the little donkey
took the road to Jerusalem. Soon
they came to a soldier standing
guard at a splendid palace.

"Have you seen a donkey with
a man and a woman?" Rebecca
asked the soldier.

"Yes, they passed this way," the
soldier answered. "Now hurry
along. There are important
visitors here to see King Herod."

Rebecca and the little donkey continued on their way. In time, they
met some shepherds keeping watch over their flocks.
"Have you seen a donkey with a man and a woman?" Rebecca asked them.

"Yes, they were going toward Bethlehem," the shepherds replied.

So the little donkey and Rebecca went on. Suddenly
glorious music filled the sky. And then they saw a great
star shining down on the little town of Bethlehem.

When they reached Bethlehem, they met a man
standing in the doorway of an inn. Rebecca asked if he had
seen Mary and Joseph and the donkey.

"Yes," he replied. "They wanted to stay here, but there
was no room at the inn. They went to the stable." And the
innkeeper showed Rebecca the way.

The stable was bathed in a wonderful light that shone from
the bright star above.

As Rebecca and the little donkey came near, they heard the
sweet sounds of a mother donkey braying and a little baby crying.

Rebecca and the little donkey entered the stable. And there, lying in a manger, was a newborn baby.

"What are you going to call him?" asked Rebecca.
"His name is Jesus," Mary replied.

In the days that followed, the little donkey and his mother
went with Mary and Joseph and the baby Jesus into Egypt. And
Rebecca rode home on a king's camel.

And it came to pass that Mary and Joseph returned to
Nazareth, and there Jesus grew up, with Rebecca as his friend.

FOR LITTLE ORNELLA

————————

THIS IS A BORZOI BOOK PUBLISHED BY ALFRED A. KNOPF, INC.

Copyright © 1989 by Brian Wildsmith. All rights reserved under International and Pan-American Copyright Conventions. Published in the United States by Alfred A. Knopf, Inc., New York. Distributed by Random House, Inc., New York. First published by Oxford University Press in 1989.

Library of Congress Cataloging-in-Publication Data: Wildsmith, Brian. A Christmas Story. Summary: A young donkey reunites with her mother in a Bethlehem stable and witnesses a miracle.   ISBN 0-679-80074-3   ISBN 0-679-90074-8 (lib. bdg.)   [1. Donkeys—Fiction. 2. Jesus Christ—Nativity—Fiction. 3. Christmas—Fiction] I. Title. PZ7.W647Ch 1989 [E] 89-7959 Manufactured in Hong Kong 1 2 3 4 5 6 7 8 9 10